BOOKS
AND
BRICKS

How a School Rebuilt the Community

By
Sindiwe Magona
In collaboration with Ellen Mayer
With an Afterword by Dr. Allistair Witten

Illustrated by
Cornelius Van Wright

65729345

STAR BRIGHT BOOKS
CAMBRIDGE, MASSACHUSETTS

The name Star Bright Books and the Star Bright Books logo are registered
trademarks of Star Bright Books, Inc. Please visit: www.starbrightbooks.com.
For bulk orders, please email: orders@starbrightbooks.com,
or call customer service at: (617) 354-1300.

Paperback ISBN-13: 978-1-59572-779-4
Star Bright Books / MA / 00108170
Printed in Canada / Marquis / 9 8 7 6 5 4 3 2 1

Printed on paper from sustainable forests.

Library of Congress Cataloging-in-Publication Data

Names: Magona, Sindiwe, author. | Mayer, Ellen, author.
Title: Books and bricks : how a school rebuilt the community / by Sindiwe
   Magona, in collaboration with Ellen Mayer; with an afterword by Dr.
   Allistair Witten.
Other titles: Books 'n bricks at Manyano School
Description: Cambridge Massachusetts : Star Bright Books, 2017. | Originally
   published: South Africa : David Philip Publishers, 2014 under the title,
   Books 'n bricks at Manyano School. | Summary: Residents of an impoverished
   South African town find new hope when they come together at their school
   and start a brickmaking business.
Identifiers: LCCN 2017002589 | ISBN 9781595727794 (paperback)
Subjects: | CYAC: Community life--South Africa--Fiction. | Poverty--Fiction.
   | Schools--Fiction. | Brickmaking--Fiction. | Blacks--South
   Africa--Fiction. | South Africa--Fiction.
Classification: LCC PZ7.M27375 Boo 2017 | DDC [Fic]--dc23
LC record available at https://lccn.loc.gov/2017002589

I wrote this story while Writer-in-Residence at the University of the Western Cape during 2011-2012. I am most grateful to the University of the Western Cape for supporting me in my writing.

Sindiwe Magona, 2014

PREFACE

I am pleased to have *Books and Bricks* published for young American readers, whom I enjoyed meeting and talking to during the 23 years that I lived in New York City before returning to my hometown, Cape Town in South Africa.

South Africa is one of the most, if not the most, unequal societies in the world; the gap between rich and poor is enormous, and it continues to grow.

In South Africa, as elsewhere, education is the only proven way to enable a child to escape poverty. Therefore, as schools are where education takes place, good schools are crucial, especially where poverty is rampant. No nation can advance or thrive if it does not make the education of its children a priority, and conduct it in such a way that the children get the maximum benefit from a well-designed, generously resourced, and all-inclusive educational system.

A school should be a source of pride to the community and a safe place for children. Sadly, in depressed areas where, ironically, children need the services of good schools the most, they do not have that security.

Books and Bricks: How a School Rebuilt the Community is fiction. It is, however, based on the true story of one such school. The message it carries is simple:

It's the parents who must save the schools. As the principal whose work transformed a vandalized playground into a prize-winning Centre of Excellence, explained to the parents: "If you allow the *skollies* to destroy the school, it is not only the education of your children they destroy, but also their future!"

A good school gives every child hope—hope to develop their talents and to grow up to live successful lives. Schools are the main ingredient in the stew that nourishes children and enables them to attain a full and joyful adulthood, to the benefit of the whole community. *Books and Bricks* shows how such a miracle actually happened; other schools can do the same.

Personally, having hit rock bottom in my own life at the early age of 23, I know the transformative power of education. I was dirt poor and a single parent, without a high school diploma. Education saved me and my children. Others can also escape lifelong poverty. The key, the way out, is education.

Sindiwe Magona
Cape Town, South Africa
February, 2017

CHAPTER 1

Broken Bottles

Manyano School was a scary place, no kidding! The fence had holes big enough for a grown man to run through. And grown men did.

The walls of the buildings were thirsty for paint. The buildings themselves looked scared. The school-yard was full of weeds, and junk of all sorts lay all over the place: broken bottles, crushed cans, skins from long-ago-eaten fruit, mango pips, and things you could no longer tell what they'd been before they got *vrot* on what was supposed to be our playing field.

We never played there. We were too scared of what might happen. And a lot happened there.

Sometimes, at night, *skollies* came to our school. They broke things. They stole things. And those things they didn't break or steal they threw all over the place. They messed everything up.

CHAPTER 2

The Street's Voice

But come rain or shine, we all went to school. We were too poor to dodge school. If you dodge school you need money to go to the movies, and we never had any money. Even a stroll along the beach is not much fun unless you have something to munch on. So our feet took us to school even though most of the time we didn't want to go there—didn't feel like it.

Even our parents didn't want to set foot in our school. The way Pa talked about it—"I's done school when I's a kid"—you'd think the school was a jail. Still, every morning Pa and Ma made me and Boetie go to school. And I can tell you, that school was a mess—every single day!

First thing every morning we had to sweep and clean up the schoolyard. *Ja-nee*, we didn't like that at all.

It was no fun to clean up a mess like that every day. Especially when you are flat-belly hungry at the same time. Who wants to go to a scary, messed up school?

I'm sure that's why so many kids dropped out of school. But it didn't stop there, oh no. Then they dropped into drink and drugs and crime. Others turned sour sixteen; they never celebrated sweet sixteen. They were in jail long before they celebrated their sixteenth birthdays.

That's what Ma was always saying to us. Every morning she was all crazy agitated. "Hey you, Salmina Arends! Boetie! *Wakker*-up! *Wakker*-up! You gotta go to school. You gotta get an education! Or else you goin' to getta a sour sixteen 'steada sweet sixteen."

I was only eleven and in the sixth grade, but that's Ma for you. She'd say that and I'd just look at her. Look at her and shake my head. I love my Ma, but I think sometimes she doesn't know what she's talking about.

The teachers said the same. They tried to keep us from the street. "Stay in school, Salmina," they said to me. "Get an education, Boetie," they said to my brother. Every day the teachers told us to stay in school and get an education. The new South Africa would need leaders, they said. Black children like us could become leaders. . . *if* we stayed in school.

Education would prepare us for a bright future. We would get good jobs and not be poor when we grew up. The world would be different and better.

But the street had a far stronger voice than the voices of all the teachers put together. That voice called out to us: *"Lekker, lekker, Hier! Lekker, lekker, Nou!* Fun, fun, Here! Fun, fun, Now!" It said nothing at all about any future.

CHAPTER 3

Fighting at Home

In my home, it was hard to see how any better future could ever find us.

We lived with Mr. Poor and knew him very, very well. He visited us often after Pa lost his job as a bricklayer. But when Ma also lost her job, after the white people she worked for left the country, Mr. Poor moved in with us—I mean, permanently.

Money was just a rumor in all the homes in our neighborhood. Ma and Pa talked about money in hushed, sad voices. We seldom saw money. Very, very seldom.

Although we didn't like school, we went there to get away from our homes. I know I did.

After Ma lost her job, she screamed at Pa, me, and Boetie every morning, but she was still better than Pa. Pa hardly ever said anything. Mostly he just grunted. But his face said worse than what Ma said. Much worse.

Ma was always fighting with him. Not *fight,*
fight...but with words, you know? Ma has a mouth,
especially when she's flat broke. And don't catch her
like that, with not a cent in her pocket and on top
of it, Pa's drinking too much.

"Yusef! Where you and your rubbish friends find
money to buy drink! I don't know."

To that Pa always answered, "What you want
from me, Mona?"

Always fights in our home, especially over the
weekend. But one thing they never fought about was
going to school. He and Ma made me and Boetie go
to school.

CHAPTER 4

Skinner Dag!

Maandag, skinner dag! Monday was the only day we were happy to go to school. You know that not one of us wanted to miss school on a Monday. We all liked to be early too, so we'd hear what happened at so-and-so's home over the weekend. Those stories flew around the schoolyard like a *veld* fire on Monday mornings, because that's when stuff happened in Brown Veld Township.

So, even when I wasn't feeling too good, if I had a headache or something, I would never stay home on a Monday.

Beat this.

On the very last day before school vacation started, something bigger and better than all the Monday gossip happened at our school. So-oo *lekker*!

We saw all these men in blue overalls carry boxes and boxes into the school strong room.

Ag, ja-nee! Huge boxes! Humongous boxes!

I thought it was books, even though the boxes were bigger than when books were given to our school. Bigger than any boxes I had ever seen in my entire life!

Then, classes ended early and we were told to go to the open quad—the place where we hold assembly.

Mr. Williams, our principal, stood in the middle of the quad, his arms flung out. "Manyano School is very lucky," he shouted. "And you, the students at this school, are very, very lucky!"

Us? Lucky? I eyeballed my *chommie*, Lindi. She raised her shoulders, rolling those huge brown eyes of hers.

Dof, her eyes said to me. I nodded. Lindi and I and all our *chommies* thought Mr. Williams was a little crazy.

Nice crazy, though. He was new at our school— he only started at the beginning of the year. But he did have some strange ideas!

Now, let me tell you something. If any of the other teachers had any ideas at all, we children didn't know anything about those ideas.

So, it was very strange to have a principal who had ideas and then wanted to share them with the entire school. I mean, even with all us children.

Mr. Williams cleared his throat and announced in a loud voice, "A businessman has given the school brand-new computers. Two for each classroom!"

Computers? Well, after a moment of goofy shock, the whole school just exploded. People whistled, clapped their hands, stamped their feet, ooh'd and aah'd.

It was like Christmas. *So-oo lekker!* Never mind that it was months after Christmas.

CHAPTER 5

Teachers Learning

When he thought we'd made more than enough noise, Mr. Williams put up his right hand and shushed us.

"We are among the very few township schools to have computers," he said. As if we didn't know.

Then, he gave a sly smile, like he was sharing a secret with us. He continued, "The teachers will come to school during the holidays so they can learn to use the computers. When school reopens, they'll be able to teach you."

The whole school laughed. Imagine that, teachers coming to school to learn, during the holidays too! *Ag*, it was so *snaaks*, even the teachers laughed.

I couldn't wait to get home to tell Ma and Pa the news. Ma said, "Maybe when you grow up you can be a bookkeeper and have a job in an office!" You could see she was very happy, just thinking that someday

I would have a good job. But Pa said nothing. Me, I wished it was already time to go back to school—the end of the silly holidays.

Ma and I were busy checking out the catalogs several days later and imagining what clothes I'd wear when I was a bookkeeper, when Boetie came home with a story about a break-in at the school. *Ag*, he went on and on and on about it, never mind that Ma and I were busy matching up different skirts and jackets.

Plus, break-ins were everyday things at the school. But my brother is like that, always builds mountains out of molehills.

So, after a while, I gave him my killer look to make him see his news was so uninteresting. And that shut him up real good.

CHAPTER 6

A Break-in

News spreads quickly in Brown Veld Township. But later that day Boetie's boring news was big news! Huge! Humongous! *Skollies* had cut a hole in the roof of the school's strong room. Cut a hole, and somehow crawled inside without breaking their necks.

They had taken those computers that were going to change our lives. Taken away each and every one of them! The whole lot!

When school reopened, many parents came to see the hole in the roof of the strong room. Everyone had heard about the theft of the computers they had not even seen, but wanted to hear more. It was *skinner dag* for all.

Lindi's gran said to Ma, "Mona, you won't believe it—for two whole days after the break-in the police were like ants in a cup of condensed milk at the school!"

She had watched the whole thing from her little one-room house, just opposite the school. But with all those computers floating around somewhere in our township, those *skollies* had not yet been caught.

"What a surprise," said Ma, then added, "The day our police ever catch a criminal I will eat my house, never mind my shoe!"

They both shook their heads.

CHAPTER 7

All Must Come

We were all very sad—parents and teachers too. That day, there was hardly any joking around. Even after the parents eventually left, even though the teachers were in meetings most of the time, and we hadn't seen one another for ages and there was lots to talk about. Then, during the lunch break we were told to go to the quad.

As we filed in, Mr. Williams handed out letters, one to each of us. If we had an older brother or sister, only the oldest one got it.

"Please take these home to your parents. The letters ask them to come to a meeting at the school tomorrow night. It is very important that they all come—not just the mothers. I would like the fathers to come too. Please try to persuade them to come." Mr. Williams didn't know Pa.

As soon as I got home I gave the letter to Pa.

We always give things like reports, messages, or letters from the school to Ma. But this time I made sure I gave this one to Pa and said, "The principal said he especially wants the fathers to come to this meeting. It is important." Then I gave Boetie a look that killed the words on the tip of his tongue. I saw him stop himself, frown, and his eyes ask twenty questions at the same time.

Then, suddenly, I saw that he understood what I was doing. "Wow," I thought. "My little Boetie is growing up." For once, he took a hint. I loved my brother that very minute. I really wanted Pa to go to the meeting. Of course, nothing could stop Ma. Pa looked at the letter, grunted, and gave it to Ma.

Know what? On the evening of the next day, both Ma and Pa got all dressed up and went to the meeting. I was very pleased. But of course it was Ma who came back and said something about it. Not my Pa.

CHAPTER 8

Robbing the Future

"That principal!" said Ma, pouring herself a cup of tea from the pot I'd made for them. I could see she was excited about something...and was dying to tell us all about it, too.

"I just wish more people had come to the meeting," she said with an exaggerated sigh. "We met in one of the classrooms. As people came in everyone was talking about the theft of the computers. The principal himself said that it was one of the worst things that had ever happened to the school," Ma said. "Don't you think so too, Pa? Sal, and you, Boetie?"

Pa grunted.

Boetie nodded.

Me? Suddenly, wet wood smoke filled my eyes.

Ma was totally right. Plus, now I would never learn how to use computers, and I would never be a bookkeeper for anyone.

But Ma was not sad like me. She was babbling non-stop about the meeting. She was so excited about it I could see myself there at that meeting. I felt what all those people there had felt. That's my Ma. She can make you see things you didn't see, just by the way she tells exactly how it was.

"Good evening! Good evening, ladies and gentlemen. I want to thank you all for coming. Don't be shy. Please, come up...there is plenty of room in the front!"

After Mr. Williams had made sure that everyone was seated, he took a deep breath and started.

"I asked you all to come this evening so that we can talk about helping your children. As you know, Manyano School has suffered many break-ins, thefts, and destruction of school property over the years.

He looked at them with narrowed eyes. It was quiet for a moment. Then he went on, "All the bad things the *skollies* do to Manyano School rob your children! The *skollies* are robbing your children of their future! We can't let that happen!"

He let that sink in and then said, "These are your children. They come to school to learn and prepare for their futures. We must do something to protect them."

"But how can we help?" one parent asked, speaking for all of them. "We have lots of problems ourselves!"

"Well, what are those problems?" he asked. The principal leaned forward so that he could more easily hear what was said, which he then furiously scribbled on the whiteboard.

"Many of us here are not working."

"We lost our jobs."

"And some of us can't find jobs."

The principal nodded. "Because of the recession? Times are hard and some businesses are laying off people and not hiring."

"Some of it's that," someone said.

"But also some of us have no skills," another said.

The principal looked at the list on the board, nodded his head several times and still nodding said, "For every problem, there is a solution."

CHAPTER 9

There is a Solution

Solutions to their problems?

"Even when we want to do something for ourselves," one mother said, "we have nowhere to meet to talk about what we want to do."

Someone else added, "Our old brick homes are jam crammed and busy falling apart, and some of our homes are shacks, not even built with bricks."

The principal said, "Again, I say, for every problem there is a solution."

He asked them, "What if we all come together and work to make things better for all—better for the children, better for the school and the place where it is, your homes, and better for Brown Veld township?"

Some people applauded, but there were those who said the principal was dreaming. The *skollies* would never allow that. They would never allow anything good to happen in the dumping grounds called townships.

Mr. Williams continued. "This is your school," he said to the parents. "It does not belong to the *skollies*—it belongs to you. If you stand by and let the *skollies* destroy Manyano School, the future of your children will also be destroyed. You can't let that happen."

Then he added, "We can all stand together. We can come together and use the school space to do things that will help solve our problems and help your children. You parents can use the school space for projects to make things better."

They could all use the school for projects to make thing better. All that space. And it was not just space, no. The school always had running water. It always had electricity. In their homes, these things were often not there, never had been there, or service was cut because the bill was not paid.

But now they could use the school space with its water and its electricity for their projects! And they were just parents, just ordinary men and women—not teachers or important people!

Mr. Williams let them think about that for a minute before speaking again. "I suggest you parents meet together next. Talk among yourselves about what projects might be done in the school."

"Then we can all come together again in a third meeting, and brainstorm some more." With a twinkle in his eye, he said, "You told me you had nowhere you could all meet. Well, you are welcome to hold your meetings right here in the school. I will come and unlock the building for you."

CHAPTER 10

The School for Us!

"The principal is going to unlock the school for us!"
Ma said excitedly. "In the evenings! Imagine!" Boetie
and I looked at each other. *That crazy principal!*
Ja-nee, things at Manyano School were certainly
getting interesting.

Giving Pa a look, Ma said, "I'm telling everybody
about the next meeting, Yusef!"

Pa shrugged and said, "You heard what people
were saying on the way back, Mona. The principal
is the one who went to university. So why does he
want us to come up with ideas?"

Ma could go alone to the next meeting. Pa said,
"I have no time for all this talk, talk, talk!"

Sure enough, on Sunday, Ma told everyone in
church about the parents meeting and how the
principal hoped all the parents would be there. I
saw a few people roll their eyes, thinking, "Uh-huh!"

On the evening of the parents meeting, I couldn't wait for Ma to get home. But Ma shuffled in looking like a doll with her stuffing spilling out. She plonked herself on the visitor's chair right by the door. She looked into her tea cup and let it warm her hands and didn't say much.

"A few more people tonight," she said quietly. "More confused than anything else." Her eyes said she was disappointed.

And where was Pa?

CHAPTER 11

Talking about Projects

Before the next meeting, more people were talking about this principal who said that parents could use the school for their projects. He was asking the parents to come and share their ideas so that they could do something to help the school.

Ma was all excited again as she put on her best Sunday dress for the meeting. She reminded Pa about the brainstorming that they would all do at that night's meeting with the principal.

Pa threw back his head and laughed, "Ho-ho-ho, Mona! Brain-storming, huh? And where will the *brains* come from?"

With the back of his hands, he wiped tears off his face.

Ma was determined. "We'll talk about the projects we can do at the school. I'm sure some people will have ideas."

"What kind of projects would *you* do, Mona? Make tea?" asked Pa.

"Well, at least," Ma said, "I'll learn something about brain-storming."

"Then go storm all you like," said Pa.

This time when Ma returned, she looked like she'd met and shaken hands with *Madiba,* Nelson Mandela himself. *Ja-nee,* I had never seen my Ma look that excited. This time she didn't even pick up her cup of tea. She didn't even sit down.

"The meeting was held in the quad," she said. "There were that many people. Chairs from all the classrooms were taken out into the quad, but lots of people still had to stand."

Mr. Williams propped up the big whiteboard against the wall and Ma stood on a chair so she could see everyone.

"Let's hear your ideas," he shouted to the parents. "What kind of projects do you want to do?"

Ma started laughing. "A few people made some suggestions, there was some discussion, and then suddenly someone shouted out, 'But all we know how to do, *meneer,* is lay bricks!' I think the man was making a joke, you know. Laughing at himself and all of us. Who did we think we were, after all, what did we know, really?"

"But, to everyone's surprise, the principal said 'so, why don't you make bricks?'"

"Make bricks?" came the surprised response from several people.

"Why not?" Lindi's Ma asked. She scowled and said, "Better than doing nothing all day."

"*Meneer,* could we make bricks—right here in the school yard?" asked the joker. "And sell them?"

"Yes!" said the principal. The principal reminded them that the school could be used for more than teaching young learners.

With a girlish smile on her face, Ma said, "After that people sat up straight, their eyes window-wide open. Everyone started talking fast; many there remembered they were bricklayers, plasterers, and welders before they were laid off."

"With those skills, you could make bricks," said Ma's friend Lizzie.

"With those bricks, we could make our small houses bigger!" said Pa's friend Gert. And someone else added, "And mend the houses that need repairs!" Getting carried away, Lizzie said, "Even build houses so that people don't have to live in shacks!"

Not believing, neighbor Abubakar looked at the principal and shouted, "Meneer, could we make the bricks right here—in the school yard?"

CHAPTER 12

Brickmaking Project

Beat this! A few days after that meeting, strange machines arrived at the school. The teachers took us out to the schoolyard and taught us the names of the machines. There was a brickmaking machine, a cement mixer, and a kiln for baking the bricks. Lots of materials came as well. Bags and bags of cement, and heaps of sand.

The very next day, the fathers fell over one another. They all wanted to make bricks. In no time at all, the schoolyard was full of stuff, full of grown-ups too. Then there was the water gurgling, mixing everything up. Suddenly, our schoolyard was *wakker. Alive!*

34

CHAPTER 13

Jobs for Workers

The real surprise for me came on the second day of the project—the most *lekker* thing of all—there was Pa! Wearing his just-washed overalls, carrying his lunch pail. *That Pa!* I fought back tears. I was that happy.

Of course, the *skollies* had to take a chance, they were so used to messing up the school. But some of the fathers stood watch by the school gate and kept them away. Some fathers even took turns being night watchmen for the school.

Then one day towards evening, after most people had left, Pa surprised a *skollie* busy carrying whole bags of cement away, using one of the wheelbarrows from the schoolyard, *nogal!*

I heard Pa tell his friend Gert about it on the phone. "You know those cowards, Gert," he said. "As soon as I blocked his way and wrestled the wheelbarrow from his hands, he started to scream like a little boy at the dentist!"

The next morning, Mr. Williams announced at assembly, "Mr. Yusef Arends is our hero!"

My heart was thumping. I was so proud! I looked at Boetie. Boetie's eyes shone like he wanted to cry. I guess happiness can make you cry, too.

The fathers were not paid real wages. Just what Ma called "steep end" wages. But "steep end" was better than nothing. Now, Mr. Poor didn't stay at our house all the time. Pa was very, very happy to get the steep end. And so was Ma, happy for him.

But if you think I was happy seeing Pa work like that, you should have seen Boetie. He went around with his chest puffed up; you'd think Pa was Tata Mandela. "See my Pa operating the cement mixer?" He'd say to anyone who would listen. Boetie loved that word 'operating.'

Soon the sound of the cement mixer became familiar to our ears. SHHLAP-SHHLOP-WHIRR. The big, tilted, open drum contraption—the cement mixer—went round and round. We could smell wet cement, a cold, thick, noisy smell. And see rows and rows of green-gray bricks—all neatly laid out on the ground—getting rock hard. They changed color when they were dry, turning just plain gray, hard and strong. To see all this was so-oo *lekker*. And to see our parents working. Pa standing there in his work clothes. Busy. Working. My Pa!

CHAPTER 14

Selling Bricks

Know what? Within a few weeks, people were buying our bricks.

All around the school and beyond, houses got rooms added to them or those busy falling apart got repaired. Some shacks were even torn down, and brick houses built instead.

You know how Lindi's Gran lived in this one-room little house, *né?* Well, past tense! She got some of the men to come and build another room for her. She bought our bricks, of course. Lindi and I visited every day to see the men work and *our* room became real.

Lindi's Gran said that we made too much noise when Lindi visits her and I visit Lindi.

"Now, I can watch my soapies in peace," she said. And now we can *skinner* all we like, with no worry about Gran's sharp ears hearing our business—*hah!*

When people started buying our bricks, Pa and

the other workers were paid some wages. The brick-making business taught people how to make bricks. It gave skills to people who didn't have any.

The principal talked to business leaders who needed workers, and they gave jobs to the people who had learned how to make bricks in our schoolyard—REAL jobs.

But now there was a new problem; when parents got jobs, there was nowhere they could leave their young children. Everyone remembered what the principal had said: "For every problem, there is a solution." He had also said: "Use the school!"

With bricks from the project, parents built a new building right next to the classrooms—a preschool! *Ag, ja-nee*, now along with SHHLAP-SHHLOP-WHIRR we heard WA-WA-WA.

But not only a preschool. At night, the same rooms were used for computer classes for our parents. COMPUTER CLASSES!!!! *Yes! Computer classes!*

CHAPTER 15

More Computers!

Dof. Not the *same* computers! But the businessman who had given us those computers the *skollies* stole and the police never found, heard about the brick making at Manyano School and came to see for himself. He saw how busy the grown-ups were, the whole day, here in our schoolyard. He saw all the machines and all the tools.

He saw how these things were safe. Well, when he saw all that, he returned the next day, along with a huge humongous truck loaded full of brand new computers. He gave the school computers—*Again!*

Mr. Williams didn't know I saw him, but there he was dancing by himself in his office, after the boxes were unloaded.

Now we had computers for the grown-ups and for the classrooms.

I was the first kid at school the next morning. My teacher was just plugging in a computer, all shiny silver gray. "Switch it on, Salmina." She smiled. I was so nervous I touched the start button so softly my hand felt like a feather on it. But the computer lit up. *I had touched a computer. I was the first child in the entire school to ever do that!* I wasn't going to wash my hands for a whole week!

Ma was the first to sign up for the grown-up computer classes. When she finished the classes, she got a real job in a shoe factory. Of course she works on a computer there. She helps count how many hours people work and helps figure out their wages on the computer.

With Ma and Pa's wages coming into our home, Mr. Poor took his bags and moved right out of our home.

CHAPTER 16

New Entrepreneurs

One thing led to another. *Ag,* it was so *snaaks*—all the kids wanted to make bricks! The teachers had to shoo us away from the machines. But we still learned something because the teachers taught us about how you start and run a business. "Entrepreneurship," it's called. *Ja-nee,* now I will have a big problem when I grow up. Which job will I do? Bookkeeper, as Ma suggested, or entrepreneur? I think I like entrepreneur better. It's not a word everybody knows, *né?*

Manyano School is now a *lekker, lekker* place. The kids here are all starry-eyed: no kidding.

The fence is mended and strong. And grown men are always in the schoolyard. Grown women too. They are there during the day. They are there well into the night. They don't come through any holes in the fence but walk in right through the gate, normal like.

The only men who do not come here, who know they are not welcome, are the ones who used to come in through the holes in the fence, the *skollies.*

Oh yes, the school has stopped being a playground for *skollies.*

Stopped.

The walls smile, painted bright, and the bustling yard is so different from what it used to be. No rubbish busy getting *vrot* in schoolyard these days.

In fact, no rubbish anywhere in sight.

Can you believe it?

Ja-nee, a lot still happens in our schoolyard, but now all of it is good stuff. Learning happens here. You see books everywhere.

But brickmaking also happens here too: so you see bricks too. Everywhere.

And, guess what? Now it's the voice of the school that calls out to us—calls to the children and the parents too—*"Lekker, lekker, hier! Lekker, lekker, Nou! Fun, fun here! Fun, fun, now!"*

AFTERWORD
By Dr. Allistair Witten
The Story Behind *Books and Bricks*

This fictional story about Manyano School and Salmina is inspired by real events at Zerilda Park Primary School in Cape Town, shortly after the historic democratic elections in 1994 that ended apartheid, the racial segregation and discrimination system in South Africa. With Nelson Mandela as our first president, it was a time of great hope, expectancy, and a bit of anxiety. We imagined what our new country, new democracy would look like, and what role everyone would play in building a non-racial society.

During the years of enforced racial segregation, the education of black children—and by this I mean African, Colored (a term used in South Africa for mixed race), and Indian children—was designed to keep them in subservient positions in society. Schools, such as Manyano School in this story, that were located in segregated non-white areas had few facilities. They lacked necessary resources needed to provide students much beyond a basic education. In addition, the majority of black schools were located in poor communities where the social challenges of poverty, hunger, ill-health, and drug abuse were rampant.

I was the principal of Zerilda Park Primary School during the brickmaking project. As teachers, parents, and community members, we realized that the school had an important role to play in building our new democracy. We understood that our school had to prepare students to become the future leaders of the country. In order to do this, we had to focus on teaching and learning, while also addressing some of the challenges that prevented our students from getting a good education. We believed that we should not wait for help to come from the outside—change had to start with us.

Zerilda Park Primary School is situated in an area of Cape Town known as Lavender Hill on the Cape Flats. This area was established by the apartheid government as a high-density housing development on the sandy outskirts of the city.

It was for the relocation of non-white residents from District Six, who were forcibly removed from their homes. District Six was a vibrant, cosmopolitan community of Black, Colored, and White residents in the heart of Cape Town, but it was declared a white only area, as part of the racial segregation policies of the time. The Cape Flats, a barren sandy area about 20 miles from the city of Cape Town, is far from work opportunities in the city and lacked community facilities like parks, sports fields, and libraries.

At the time of this story, Zerilda Park Primary School had 1,104 students and 29 teachers, including me, the principal. The school served the communities of Lavender Hill and Vrygrond (the Afrikaans word for "free ground"). Vrygrond was an informal settlement, where isiXhosa and Afrikaans speaking families who did not have formal homes lived in shacks made from corrugated tin and found materials. Most of the students at the school were Colored; none were white. The school had Afrikaans, English, and isiXhosa-speaking students, with Afrikaans and English as the languages of instruction.

At Zerilda Park Primary School we knew that learning needed to take place in a safe environment, free of danger or fear. For this to happen, we had to find ways to address the challenges that confronted us at school. We saw the school as a community asset. It was not only a place where the students could learn, but also where families could be supported.

The brick- and block-making project as it was called—the project made concrete blocks in addition

to bricks—was one of a number of projects that we started at the school and formed part of a program called, "Building a Better Life." We also had a computer training project, just as in the story. The brick- and block-making project was set up to provide employment opportunities and skills training for parents, and also for young people who were without work, some like the *skollies* in this story. We understood that this activity, while it strengthened families and created a greater sense of community ownership of the school, was not the core work of the school. The core work remained teaching and learning, which was our primary responsibility.

In order to implement the project, we had to build partnerships with others who could help us. A church minister in the community managed the brick- and block-making project, and a local technical college provided the initial training to those working on the project. Business students at the University of Cape Town developed the business plans, and the funds to buy the equipment were donated by the embassy of a European country and a national retail company. Building these partnerships took time, and there were many times when our proposals were turned down.

Eventually we got the project up and running in the schoolyard. Besides using the bricks and

blocks to build a preschool on the school grounds, bricks for construction elsewhere in the city were sold. The project paid workers a stipend and skilled workers trained new ones in the brick- and block-making processes. Many families also bought bricks to build, extend, or renovate their own homes. During this time, the government was giving people in the townships subsidies to help them build homes, so families had this money to draw on. As news of the project spread, building contractors also bought the bricks and blocks.

The brick- and block-making project affected the school and community in a number of ways. Parents and community members felt connected to the school and became more interested in its activities. They began to attend meetings in greater numbers to discuss school and community matters. Incidents of burglaries and vandalism at the school came to an end as parents and community members started to care about the school and see it as an important community asset. Students at the school also studied the project as an example of social entrepreneurship. The course included topics like the manufacturing process, market demand and supply, and budgeting. Students could go onto the site to study the full production cycle that started with raw materials like sand, stone, cement, and water, to the delivery of the end product to the market.

The most important effect of the project on the community, however, was the sense of dignity and pride it gave to those working on it. The project ran for about four years and won a national Impumelelo

Award in 2000 for contributing to poverty reduction and community development.

The brick- and block-making project was not the only activity going on at the school. Students participated in science and environment projects, as well as mathematics and art competitions. The school started its own jazz band that eventually performed at the famous Baxter Theatre in Cape Town. Sports were also an important part of life at the school and it produced students who competed at provincial and national levels. Zerilda Park Primary School became a hive of activity for students, families, and community members. It was a place where students wanted to be. It was a place of learning and a place of fun. And it was safe.

Many years have passed since South Africa's first democratic elections. The promise of schools to provide all children and young people with a good education—especially those in the country's urban and rural township communities—remains unfulfilled.

Too many students drop out before they reach the end of high school. In many of the poor communities, unemployment and poverty have increased, as have the problems associated with them. All of these problems affect student learning, and must be addressed if we want our young people to thrive in our democracy.

Schools on their own cannot address the many challenges that face education in South Africa. Schools will only succeed if parents and communities get involved and support them. Fortunately, there are schools like Zerilda Park Primary School all over South Africa. They succeed in providing their students with a good education despite tremendous challenges. They build clinics to deal with health challenges, establish food gardens to feed hungry students, train parents to develop skills and get jobs, and focus on improving teaching and learning to ensure student success. These schools call themselves "community schools." There is much we can learn from what they are doing—in South Africa and also in other countries–and all of us should support them.

School should be a place where students feel safe and cared for. It should be a place where hard work and commitment are encouraged. And it should be a place where our children can dream their futures— just like Salmina here—and know that these futures can be achieved because their teachers and parents care and believe in them.

Dr. Allistair Witten
Adjunct Professor at the Bertha Center for Social Innovation and Entrepreneurship at the Graduate School of Business, University of Cape Town

Dr. Allistair Witten has been involved in the field of education for over 30 years, and has more than 20 years of experience as a teacher and principal in township schools in Cape Town. He was the founding Director of the Centre for the Community School at the Nelson Mandela Metropolitan University in South Africa.

Dr. Witten was also responsible for the design and implementation of the School Leadership Initiative—a collaboration between Harvard University and the University of Johannesburg to train school and district leaders in South Africa. Dr. Witten has extensive practice-based and training experience in the areas of school leadership and management, organizational change and development, and systemic school improvement. The current focus of his work is on developing the concept of the community school in South Africa where he facilitated the establishment of the Manyano Network of Community Schools, which is aimed at encouraging greater parental and community involvement in schools.

GLOSSARY

Afrikaans words in the story: *Afrikaans is one of the eleven official languages in South Africa. It is derived from 17th century Dutch.*

Ag: oh

Boetie: little brother

Chommie: friend, chum

Dag: day

Dof: stupid, slow to understand

Hier: here

Ja-nee: indeed, O.K.

Lekker: nice, cool, great

Maandag: Monday

Meneer: Sir

Né?: not so?

Nogal: on top of that, quite, fairly,

Nou: now

Skinner: gossip

Skollies: vandals, gang members

Snaaks: funny

Veld: field

Vrot: rotten

Wakker: awake, active

OTHER INFORMATION

Madiba: South African leader Nelson Mandela's clan name, by which he is often and fondly called.

Manyano: Xhosa word meaning "coming together, unity"; isiXhosa is one of the official languages in South Africa.

The new South Africa: Post-apartheid South Africa, after the country's first democratic elections in 1994.

Tata ("Tata Mandela"): Father, term of respect and endearment used for Nelson Mandela by younger people.

Township: The urban areas that, during apartheid, were where nonwhites had to live. Townships were usually built on the edge of a city or town.

Veld: field, pasture, vegetation

Apartheid: Until 1993, South Africa had always had a white minority government that enforced laws of racial segregation. In 1948, the newly elected all-white government introduced a more stringent policy of racial segregation and political and economical discrimination, apartheid, including the Group Areas Act, that declared where people were or were not allowed to live.

AFRICA

SOUTH AFRICA

NELSON MANDELA

Nelson Mandela is the man who transformed South Africa from an oppressive racial society into a liberal democratic modern state.

He was born in 1918 in the eastern Cape, a child of the Madiba Xhosa clan. He attended a local school and from there he studied law at the University of Fort Hare and the University of the Witwatersrand in Johannesburg. At this liberal, free-thinking establishment, he was influenced by the prevailing

attitudes of equality. Everywhere else he saw discrimination and racism.

In 1943, Mandela joined the ANC (African
National Congress), a movement founded in 1912
supporting Black equality and advancement. He was
among the first African lawyers in South Africa and
knew firsthand about the hardships imposed on the
non-white population by the racist government. He
rose to a high position in the ANC.

The Nationalist Party won the white-only election
in 1948, and established the Apartheid (Separate
Development) system of racial segregation and
discrimination. The ANC vigorously opposed white-
only government. The government banned the ANC
and declared it illegal.

In 1956, Mandela was one of 155 people accused
of treason. Their trial lasted until 1961 when all
were acquitted.

Mandela now realized that armed struggle was
inevitable, and the uMkhonto weSizwe (Spear of
the Nation) was formed to carry on the struggle
underground. It was not very effective against an
organized police state.

In 1963, the Security Police raided the Headquar-
ters of uMkhonto weSizwe, and the local ANC and
arrested everyone found there.

As it happened Mandela was not there but was later arrested, and along with ten other leaders, put on trial. This is known as the Rivonia Trial, and Mandela was named "Accused Number One."

The trial went on for months; it was expected that if any of the leaders were found guilty, the death penalty would be imposed. To everyone's relief, jail sentences were given; Mandela was sentenced to life in jail. At the end of the trial, Mandela made a speech that is still often quoted:

"During my lifetime I have dedicated myself to this struggle of the African people. I have fought against white domination, and I have fought against black domination. I have cherished the ideal of a democratic and free society in which all persons live together in harmony and with equal opportunities. It is an ideal which I hope to live for and to achieve. But if needs be, it is an ideal for which I am prepared to die."

Mandela spent 27 years in jail on Robben Island with some of the other Rivonia accused. While there, he became an icon and famous around the world as people agitated to "Free Mandela" and South Africa became increasingly reviled.

But things changed in South Africa. In 1989, F.W. de Klerk became President; within months all underground movements were unbanned. Mandela was released from prison. In 1993, Mandela and de Klerk were jointly awarded the Nobel Prize for Peace.

The following year the first democratic elections were held, and the ANC won. Mandela became the first Black President of South Africa. He believed in—and practiced—"Forgive and Forget."

Nelson Mandela retired in 1999 and thereafter kept a low profile. He passed away in 2013 at age 95, revered and appreciated. In tribute, United States President Barack Obama said, "He no longer belongs to us; he belongs to the ages."

Will we see his like again?

DISCUSSION QUESTIONS

1. How can the loss of jobs impact a community? How can it change families?

2. Is getting a good education important? Why?

3. What are some of the problems facing Manyano School?

4. Why do Ma and Pa make sure that Salmina and Boetie go to school every day?

5. Salmina says that Mr. Poor lives with her family. What does she mean by this?

6. Do you think it was a good idea for Mr. Williams to involve the parents in the school meetings? Why? Why does he especially want the fathers to come?

7. How does Mr. Williams change the way the parents and children think of Manyano School?

8. Mr. Williams states that the skollies are stealing the children's futures. What does he mean by this?

9. Mr. Williams wants the Manyano School to be open to not just the students, but also to all of Brown Veld Township. How does this help to build a connection between the school and the larger community?

10. The brickmaking project created many changes in Brown Veld Township. Discuss or draw a diagram of the positive consequences that grow from this one activity within the community.

11. Discuss the idea of personal and community pride. Find some examples within the story. What are examples from your own community? Can you think of a project that your school can do with your community?

12. How does Salmina change from the beginning of the book to the end of the book?

13. How do Ma and Pa change from the beginning of the book to the end of the book?

14. Salmina decides she may want to be an entrepreneur when she grows up. What does this mean? What would you like to do when you are older?

15. Is Salmina's school different from your school? In what way is it similar to your school or different?

16. What did you learn about South Africa that you didn't know before you read this book?

17. Which American reminds you of Nelson Mandela? Why?

Sindiwe Magona grew up in South Africa under apartheid. Although she was a qualified primary school teacher, she was unable to obtain a position and became a domestic worker to support her three children. She later earned a B.A. from the University of South Africa and a master's degree from Columbia University. She worked for the United Nations for 23 years. A prolific author of novels, poetry, and children's books, Magona's writing reflects her experiences with poverty, single-parenthood, racism, teaching, and social activism. She has won South Africa's highest literary awards as well as a Lifetime Achievement Award for contributions to South African literature. She currently lives in Cape Town, South Africa.

photo: Mindaugas Sereiva

Ellen Mayer is a children's book author and early literacy educator. She has conducted research at Harvard University on parental and community involvement in schools. She holds an M.Phil in Sociology from Columbia University and lives in Cambridge, Massachusetts.